What Adirondack kids are saying...

"This is a very exciting book. I love camping because it's always an adventure and this is like that. It's a great adventure." — *K. Payne, 7th Lake*

"This book is very funny and adventurous." — *J. Newton, Inlet*

"It was a very exciting book. I liked the part when Nick dropped the ping-pong balls...." — *M. Levi, Limekiln Lake*

"The story was... long on adventure. I felt scared when the Adirondack kids felt they were lost." — *A. Frey, Inlet*

"It was funny when the kids were walking up the mountain and Justin started to panic..." — *J. Anderson, Limekiln*

"I liked the part when it sounded like Nick was falling off a cliff, but he was only falling two feet!" — *S. Payne, 6th Lake*

The Adirondack Kids® #2

Rescue on Bald Mountain

The Adirondack Kids® #2
Rescue on Bald Mountain

Justin & Gary VanRiper
Copyright © 2002. All rights reserved.

First Paperback Edition, February 2002
Second Paperback Printing, June 2002
Third Paperback Printing, May 2003
Fourth Paperback Printing, September 2004
Fifth Paperback Printing, June 2006

Cover illustration by Susan Loeffler
Illustrated by Glenn Guy

Published by
Adirondack Kids Press
39 Second Street
Camden, New York 13316

Printed in the United States of America
by Patterson Printing, Michigan

ISBN 0-9707044-1-0

To Elizabeth, Gabrielle & Brett, Reading will always take you to new heights!

The
Adirondack
Kids® #2

Rescue on Bald Mountain

Josh

Gary VanRiper

by
Justin & Gary VanRiper
Illustrations by Glenn Guy

Adirondack Kids Press
Camden, New York

Other Books
by Justin and Gary VanRiper

The Adirondack Kids®

The Adirondack Kids® #3
The Lost Lighthouse

The Adirondack Kids® #4
The Great Train Robbery

The Adirondack Kids® #5
Islands in the Sky

The Adirondack Kids® #6
Secret of the Skeleton Key

Other Books
by Justin VanRiper

The Adirondack Kids® Story & Coloring Book
Runaway Dax

Justin & Dax

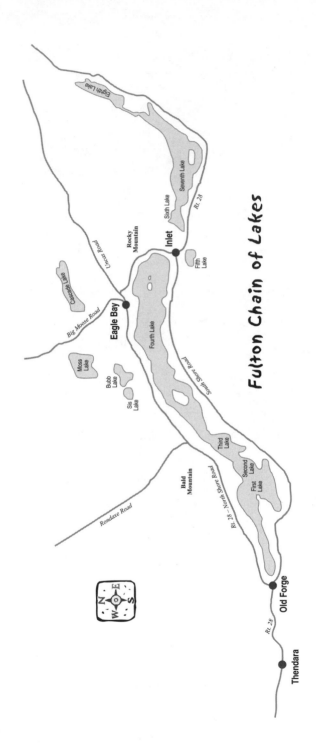

Contents

In Memory
For Bobby
(1955-1963)

my uncle - JVR
my brother - GVR
like no other

chapter one

The Quest

Justin Robert was clinging to the hand of his friend with all his might.

"I'm falling!" yelled Nick. "Don't let me go!"

Justin was panting and speaking out between uneven breaths. "I'm trying to hold you – you're slipping – I can't help it," he said. "Get a hold – use your feet."

"I can't," cried Nick. He sounded desperate. "My sneaks aren't touching anything." His sweaty fingers suddenly slipped through Justin's grasp.

Nick and Justin locked eyes as Nick lurched backwards and fell helplessly away from the rock face through the air – all two and a half feet to the ground below. He groaned and stood up, brushing pine needles off the back of his shorts and shirt.

"That was pathetic," said Jackie. She stood at the base of the small boulder with her hands on her hips. "You two wouldn't last five minutes climbing a high peak."

Justin glared down at her. "We're not trying to climb a high peak," he said. "Just this one big old

1

"I'm falling," yelled Nick. "Don't let me go!"

rock." He scooped up his green bucket hat and jumped down to join them.

Nick Barnes and Jackie Salsberry were Justin's best friends. They spent every summer together on Fourth Lake in the Adirondack Mountains. It was Fourth of July weekend and the three Adirondack kids were on a special mission.

"We have one more day to help Nick get over his fear of heights," said Jackie.

Nick hung his head and moaned. "I wish I'd never won that plane ride," he said.

"Well, I'm glad you did," said Justin. Nick could pick two people to join him in the flight. Rather than his mom and dad, he chose Justin and Jackie. "It's going to be so cool, looking down on Fern Park and watching a thousand ping-pong balls drop all over the field."

Nick frowned. "Stop talking about looking down," he said. "All the kids will just look like teeny tiny ants, anyway. We won't even see the balls hit the ground."

Justin knew his friend was scared, but he couldn't stop himself from rubbing it in. "I heard the pilot has to fly upside down," he said. "That way all the balls can pour out of the window."

"Cut it out, Justin," said Nick. "I mean it, or you're not invited, and the only ping-pong balls you'll see are the ones popping you on the head."

"So what," said Justin. "Then I'll just turn them in at the prize stand and win a bunch of neat stuff while you're a billion miles up in the air turning green."

It was the closest the two friends had come to having their first major summer fight. Jackie saw the blow-out coming, and interrupted them. "I'm telling you, the best way for Nick to overcome his fear of heights is to climb Bald Mountain," she said. "It's not too hard and the views are fantastic." She looked straight at Nick. "And it's *safe*."

Jackie had climbed Bald Mountain several times. Justin had once. But Nick had always avoided it. In fact, he had bunk beds in his room and had never used the top bunk.

"I don't know..." Nick said.

"That's a maybe, and maybe is yes," said Jackie. "It's settled then. We'll pack tonight and climb in the morning."

Nick moaned.

"Now what's wrong?" asked Justin. "You're not going to chicken out, are you?" With arms bent at the elbows, he moved them back and forth like flapping wings and bobbed his head up and down. "*Bawwwk- bawk-bawk-bawk.*"

"No," said Nick, defensively. "I'll do it." He reached into his back pocket and pulled out a candy bar with chocolate oozing from each end of the package. "Smushed," he said.

Justin still couldn't help it. "Just think," he said, and grinned. "Tomorrow, that could be you."

chapter two

Sword Play

"Let's go to Pioneer Village," said Justin. "I'll stop by camp and get my sword."

"Mine is already there," said Nick. "And this time I get to be the Black-and-Silver Knight."

"No," said Justin. "I am always the Black-and-Silver Knight. You can be the Rainbow Knight. Or the Indigo Knight. Or the..."

"Good night," said Jackie, with disgust. "If you two are going to play more of that medieval stuff, I'm heading back to the island."

Jackie was a native Adirondack kid. She lived summers on Salsberry Island on Fourth Lake. During the school year, she lived with her family in a winterized cabin on the mainland. She headed for her small silver motorboat, the one they called the putt-putt, tied at the Roberts' dock.

Nick called out to her. "Hey Jackie, don't go," he said. "You can be the Pink Knight."

"And how would you like to be the Black-and-*Blue* Knight?" asked Jackie. She untied the ropes and jumped into the boat. "I'll see you in a little while. Be ready to pack." The engine erupted with the pull of a cord, and she was quickly out into open water, headed for home.

Pioneer Village was a small community located in the trees between the two boys' camps. Every year all three friends rebuilt their stores and homes with walls of sticks and held special meetings high above the town on a large boulder they called, *The Rock*.

Earlier in the week, Justin and Nick had decided Pioneer Village would become a Medieval Village – at least when Jackie wasn't playing with them. Instead of having a mayor, they took turns being the king's guardian. The General Store became the Silversmith Shoppe, tended by knights in training.

"Here is your armor, Great Knight," said Nick. He handed Justin what was left of the cradle from an ancient, broken wheelbarrow.

"Thank you, my squire," said Justin. He took the small scrap of metal fitted with two pieces of rope and strapped it to his body, positioning it as a breast plate. Then he picked up his cardboard shield and a sword, the one he bought in South Carolina when he was on vacation. Painted silver and black, the wooden sword looked real. "Put on your helmet and we shall fight," he said. "Prepare to be taught a lesson from the Black-and-Silver Knight."

A noise distracted Justin from behind. "Who goes there," he said loudly, and spun away from Nick. "It is a spy," he yelled, and pointed his sword

6

at a little eastern chipmunk that appeared on a fallen log. He thrust his sword forward. "Get thee gone, unwelcome intruder, or face my blade!"

The chipmunk sat up, glanced at Justin, and ate a nut.

Nick took the opportunity to put on his helmet, a large plastic watering can that he propped on his head upside down, its long spout pointing out and forward in front of his face. Unable to find his sword, he picked up a large stick for a weapon.

Caw, Caw, Caw. A crow soared overhead and landed on a branch in the canopy directly above the two warriors.

"Ah, it is my loyal falcon, Merlyn," cried Nick. "Fly down here and help me, my faithful servant. I command you."

The crow flew away.

Justin turned back to face Nick.

The sword and the stick clashed in the air.

Small pieces of bark flew from Nick's stick. "Hey, not so hard," he said.

"Silence," said Justin, and struck out again. This time Nick's frail weapon snapped in half.

Nick bent over, scooped up a combination of pine needles and dirt and tossed it through the air into the direction of his opponent.

"Nice try," said Justin, as he ducked and closed his eyes to avoid the flying debris. "Now take *that.*" With eyes still closed, Justin swung his sword a little too close to his friend's head and hit the spout.

Nick's helmet spun around sideways and dropped down fully over his head. It stuck, and he couldn't see. He staggered, bumped into a tree and fell backwards onto the ground.

"Sorry," said Justin. "I didn't mean to come so close to you." He reached out and helped his friend to his feet. "Are you all right?"

Nick removed the helmet from his head. "That's okay," he said. It was the second time in less than three hours he was wiping pine needles from his clothes. He reached into his back pocket and frowned. "I've got to stop carrying candy bars this way."

The two boys tossed their weapons into the Silversmith Shoppe and walked up to *The Rock*.

Justin sat down and used the front of his shirt to wipe sweat from his forehead. The woods were still.

Nick flopped next to him onto the large flat boulder in a heap. He rolled onto his back and stared blankly up through the trees.

"I think I have an idea on how to keep you from being scared of hiking up Bald Mountain," Justin said, quietly.

Nick sounded doubtful. "How?"

"We'll just pretend it's a real medieval adventure," Justin said. His voice grew bolder. "The tower on the mountain can be where the evil king keeps his prisoners." He stopped and thought for a moment. Then his eyes brightened. "We have to climb the castle walls to get to the top and save the good king's daughter."

Nick sat up. He looked hopeful. "Yeah, and the good king has to give us a big reward."

The two friends laughed, slapped a high five, then went silent. There was a steady and familiar hum rising from the lake.

Justin and Nick jumped to their feet and ran to meet Jackie in her putt-putt at the dock.

chapter three

A Careful Plan

It was dusk. The early summer sky still glowed and reflected off the lake when Justin, Nick and Jackie gathered around the Roberts' kitchen table.

Jackie glanced out the large picture window where silhouettes of tree trunks in the front yard formed wide vertical lines against the silver surface of the water. "It might rain in the morning," she said. "If it does, the rocks will be too slippery and we'll have to wait until later in the day to hike when it's dry."

Justin's mom set a platter with fresh home-baked sugar cookies in the center of the table, along with three tall glasses of milk. There were bears, loons, deer, moose and a few shapes no one could recognize, each smothered with colorful frosting. Some had sprinkles.

"I think I know which ones Justin made," said Nick. Avoiding the mystery shapes, his hand was the first to plunge into the small pile of frosted animals.

"Remember, Jackie is in charge of this little expedition up Bald Mountain," Mrs. Robert said. "She is the one with wilderness training, and what she says – goes."

"I know mom, we'll listen," said Justin. Mrs. Robert left the room.

"I can't believe you baked cookies when it's a million degrees outside," Nick said. "But I'm glad you did!" He bit the head off a loon to get at the red cinnamon eye, and closely examined the remaining body of the bird. "I'b neber seen bwack fwaustig befour," he mumbled, with his mouth full. Then the loon was gone.

"Don't eat all of them," Justin said. He knew Nick could do a lot of damage to a big plate of cookies in a small amount of time. "Mom and I worked all morning to make these. I want some of them for the hike."

"Yes, let's talk about our list," said Jackie. "Here's what we need to bring."

Nick interrupted. "I'll pack the candy," he said, and devoured a bear. "And some of these cookies."

"But I'll bring the peanut butter cups," Justin said.

Jackie looked frustrated. "You guys, this is serious," she said. "We have to take plenty of water and some first-aid supplies."

Nick's eyes widened. "First- aid supplies!" he said. "You said this hike was going to be safe!"

"It is going to be safe," Jackie said. "But you still need to be careful and be prepared. You don't want to dehydrate, do you?"

Nick stood up and pointed the antler of a moose right at her. "You said not to worry," he said. "Now you're saying we'll be up so high we could have all the air sucked out of us."

Justin sat quietly and munched on another cookie. He was glad it was Jackie's turn to deal with Nick.

"Not deflated, *dehydrated*," said Jackie, with dismay. "When you sweat and run out of water, you can get cramps or even heatstroke. People can live for weeks without candy bars and cookies. But you always need plenty of water."

"Cramps? Stroke?" Nick sat down and slumped his head forward into his arms on the table and groaned.

"Listen," Jackie said. "Have either of you ever heard of Chrissy Wendell?"

Nick lifted his head and looked at Justin. Justin shrugged.

"Chrissy Wendell is the first dog to ever become a 46er," she said.

Nick looked confused. "A dog played football," he said. "What has that got to do with climbing a mountain?"

Jackie looked like she was going to cry.

"C'mon, Nick," said Justin. He hated it when Jackie got so upset. "Not a 49er – a 46er." He looked at Jackie and tried to encourage her. "I didn't even think about animals climbing all 46 of the Adirondack's high peaks. That's pretty cool."

Jackie remained composed, and looked over at

Nick. "If a dog can climb 46 peaks that are 4000 feet high or higher, you can climb one little mountain with a well-marked trail," she said. "It doesn't even take an hour to get to the top."

"And it has one of the most beautiful vistas not only along the Fulton Chain, but in the entire Adirondack Park," said Mrs. Robert, as she reentered the kitchen. "Let's wrap this up now. It is getting late and you all have a big day tomorrow. I called Mrs. Barnes. She will drop you off on her way to do some errands in Old Forge, and then pick you up on her way back to Eagle Bay."

Jackie quickly assigned from her list the items each one would be responsible to carry up the mountain in small day packs. Nick would bring a map and some rain gear. "You never know when it's going to storm in the mountains," she said. "Justin, you bring a whistle. And even though we are leaving early enough in the day and shouldn't need it, bring a flashlight, too."

Justin nodded.

"I'll bring the first-aid kit and my field guide," Jackie said.

They would all bring water.

Justin said good-night to his friends as they pushed through the screen door and hurried down the steps of the front porch. Jackie stuffed her list back into her pocket, and Nick, with a small bag of cookies in his hand, was still nibbling on a bear as they disappeared into the night.

A surge of cool mountain air filled Justin's lungs as he stood in the doorway and breathed in deeply. Then he sighed.

"Are you all right, Justin?" asked Mrs. Robert. She wrapped her arms around him and squeezed him tightly.

Justin smiled quickly. "Yes, Mom, great." He gave her a quick kiss on the cheek and headed up the stairs to the sleeping porch.

chapter four

The Journey Begins

Justin woke up to the sound of rain gently tapping on the roof directly above his head. It was late morning. His parents had let him sleep in. He had needed it. The sun was out now and overpowering the dying drizzle.

Justin pulled on his clothes that were carefully set out the night before on a chair next to his bed. He could hear his parents in the kitchen below. Their voices became clearer as he slowly walked down the stairs.

"It's going to be a muggy day, very unusual for the mountains," said Mr. Robert. He stood at the kitchen window and pointed at the steam rising from the paved portion of the driveway. "It's burning off fast."

Mrs. Robert greeted Justin as he shuffled into the kitchen, rubbing his eyes, and dropped into a chair.

"Good morning, my little mountain climber," she said. "Have some breakfast. Nick and Jackie are on their way."

Justin came alive. "I will in a second, Mom," he said. Before she could protest, he grabbed his day pack and ran out the front screen door and across the long green lawn toward the boathouse.

"Where is your pack?" asked Mrs. Robert, when he returned to the cabin.

"It's all set to go," said Justin. He changed the subject. "Hey, Dad, what are you doing home already?"

Mr. Robert smiled and plucked a set of keys from the counter. "I finished my photo shoot at Lake Placid early and drove straight home," he said. "Nick's mom has already left for Old Forge to do her errands. I told her I would be glad to drop you kids off at Bald Mountain."

Justin woofed down a piece of toast and chugged a glass of orange juice. More sunlight poured into the kitchen window. He could feel the warmth where the rays touched the back of his blue short-sleeved shirt.

"I love that color on you," said Mrs. Robert. "It really brings out your blue eyes."

"Mom, you're embarrassing me again," said Justin. He complained whenever she complimented him, but it made him feel really good inside.

"I think it's going to be a great Fourth of July weekend after all," Mr. Robert said. "It will be hot, but there should be a lot of people climbing today."

"Don't remind me." It was Nick. He walked into the kitchen just as the front door banged shut.

"You can sure move fast when you want to," Justin said. "Hey, did you see Jackie?"

Nick nodded. "She's pulling her stuff out of the putt-putt right now," he said. "My stuff is out on the porch."

Mr. Robert helped the three friends load their gear into the jeep.

"Where's your day pack, Son?" asked Mr. Robert.

Justin hurried into the back seat. "I've got it, Dad. Let's go!"

The ride along Route 28 to the base of Bald Mountain took less than ten minutes. Several cars were already parked roadside, some with brightly colored kayaks strapped to roof carriers. One had a mountain bike standing upright in brackets.

"I've always wondered what it would be like to sit on a mountain bike when it was traveling 60 miles an hour on top of a car like that," said Nick, as he jumped out of the jeep.

Justin laughed. "Yeah, it would be a lot of fun – unless the driver forgot and pulled into the garage," he said.

"Excuse me, can we climb Bald Mountain *this* summer?" Jackie asked. She was pulling on her day pack when a colorful oversized van turned into the parking area. It looked like a huge tie-dyed t-shirt on wheels, highlighted with bright flowers, birds and peace symbols.

A large woman with long, braided hair and wearing

17

"Come along, Sarah, we're here,"
said the woman in a tie-dyed dress. "It's time
to climb the big mountain."

a long, loose tie-dyed dress and flip flops stepped out of the vehicle. The door squeaked as it opened. "Come along, Sarah, we're here," she said in a loud, cheery voice to someone inside the van. "It's time to climb the big mountain."

Jackie glanced at the woman's footwear and shook her head. "They're doomed," she said.

Mr. Robert looked at his watch. "All right you three. It's 45 minutes up and 45 minutes back down. We'll allow you about 15 minutes at the top. Either Mrs. Barnes or I will be right here waiting for you in one hour and 45 minutes." He paused. "And remember, Jackie is in charge."

"Great, Dad. Thanks," said Justin.

"Are you sure you're okay, Justin?" Mr. Robert asked.

"Positive, Dad."

Mr. Robert disappeared into the jeep.

Nick looked puzzled. "What's the matter, Justin?" he asked. "You're not sick, are you?"

"No, I'm fine," Justin said.

Mr. Robert honked the horn as he pulled out onto Route 28 and headed back toward Eagle Bay.

"I'm following Jackie," Nick said. "I'm not climbing behind someone who is sick."

"I said I'm not sick," Justin said. "Let's just stick to our plan, okay?"

"What plan?" asked Jackie.

Nick struck a dramatic pose and gestured toward the mountain as he spoke. "We are great knights and we are scaling yonder castle walls to save a princess in distress," he bellowed.

Jackie simply shook her head, and started for the trail.

chapter five

Every Hero
Has a Weakness

Jackie, Nick and Justin began to walk single file along the well-worn trail, sometimes hopping on small rocks to avoid stepping into mud. Several birds called softly from the canopy of the many tall, thin trees that towered over them. They came to a fork in a small clearing where a weathered wooden sign was tacked to a tree.

Jackie read the crudely handwritten message. "Bald Mountain Trail – Left." A small arrow on the sign pointed toward a flat, grassy pathway.

Nick looked back over his shoulder at Justin, and grinned. "This is easy," he said. "It doesn't even feel like we're going up."

Justin didn't reply. He knew what was coming.

The path gradually narrowed and the grass disappeared. Jutting rock and bare tree roots became steps as the three adventurers began weaving their way around boulders that seemed to grow larger as the trail became more steep. Some were taller than

Jackie, and she disappeared at a severe bend up the stony staircase.

Nick was puffing, and called out to her. "Let's rest here," he said. He sat down on one of the smaller boulders.

"Rest?" Jackie asked. She stepped back and pulled Nick to his feet. "We have to keep moving if we are going to stay on schedule and have time to enjoy the view on the top. Let's go."

Justin remained quiet. Sweat began to form on his forehead and all along the brim of his bucket hat. And it wasn't from the heat.

"Are you all right, Justin?" asked Jackie. "You don't look good."

Justin managed a slight smile, and shifted the day pack on his back. "I'm fine," he said.

"I told you he was sick," said Nick. "I know this isn't an official meeting, but I vote we go back now."

"Don't even think about it," said Justin, sternly. "Climb!"

Nick shrugged and fell in behind Jackie, who had stopped again and was staring off to her left. "What is it?" he asked.

"We've made better time than I thought," she said. "Look." She pointed through a small gap between several trees to a body of water that lay off on the horizon.

"Hey, look at that little pond," said Nick.

"It's not a pond," said Justin. "It's Fourth Lake." He never looked up.

"No way," said Nick. "Our lake? It's too small." He looked back at his friend. "Hey, Justin, what's wrong?"

Justin was on his knees with his eyes fixed on the earth immediately beneath him. "I can't go any further," he said, and groaned. "We have to go back."

Jackie took off her pack and sat down on the ground next to him. "But why?" she asked.

Justin looked up at Nick, meekly. "I'm really sorry I mocked you yesterday about being afraid of heights," he said. Then came the dreaded confession he had hoped he would never have to make. "Mom and Dad tried to bring me up Bald Mountain a few years ago, but I took one look out at Fourth Lake right here, and screamed all the way back to the car." He sighed and bowed his head. "I really thought I could do it this time, but I can't."

"That's okay, Justin," said Nick. "It's no big deal."

"Really, Justin, if you want to go back, we will," Jackie said. "I've already been up this mountain a bunch of times." She reached into her pack. "Let's just rest a minute and have a drink of water."

A blank look came over the two boys' faces.

Jackie looked at Nick, then at Justin, then back at Nick. "What?" she asked.

Nick answered first.

"Well, I didn't bring any water," he said. "I thought you guys would, so I brought some other stuff."

"Like what?" Jackie asked.

Nick began pawing through his pack. He picked out a few loose band-aids and his hand-held video

23

game. The pack was mainly filled with cookies and candy bars.

"Wait," he said. "If we get really thirsty, I've got some juice blasters. It's this really cool stuff that you bite down on and juice squirts out in your mouth."

"You guys," said Jackie. "I told you water was the most important thing to bring. You brought water didn't you, Justin?"

Justin shifted his pack. "Um."

"I give up," Jackie said, and raised her hands in disgust. "I thought I could trust you two." She hesitated and then tried to sneak a peek at Justin's pack. He turned his back away from her. "Well, what *did* you bring?" she asked. "More junk food?"

"Dax," Justin said, flatly.

Jackie looked confused. "What?"

"Dax," Justin repeated, without a hint of apology in his voice. "I brought Dax." The sleek, short-haired calico cat popped her head out of the pack and peered over his shoulder. It was his faithful camp companion, more accustomed to boats and water than backpacks and mountains. Justin reached up and stroked the top of her head.

"You said some dog walked up all those mountains," Justin said. "I thought if a dog can do it, then so can Dax." He pulled her out of the pack and set her next to him on the ground. Her patches of black, rufous and white acted together as camouflage. She blended in with the surroundings, especially where there were shadows.

Dax popped her head out of Justin's pack.

Before Jackie could utter a word from her wide-open mouth, a high-pitched and powerful voice boomed from the trail behind them.

"Excuse us, excuse us, coming through, coming through."

It was the lady in the tie-dyed dress. She carried a young child in a front pack and a small canvas bag in one hand. With flip flops flopping and dyed dress flapping, she marched briskly along with great determination. "My, this is a much bigger mountain than I ever imagined it was," she said to no one in particular as she rushed by. "We'll be at the top soon. Isn't the air wonderful? My, but it is hot, isn't it? Oh, look, a beautiful little butterfly."

She never stopped talking, and as quickly as she had entered their space, she was gone. The three Adirondack kids were frozen in place, slightly stunned at the sudden audio and visual assault.

Justin looked around in a panic. "Where's Dax?" he asked.

"There," said Nick. He pointed up the trail.

Dax was off and following the lady with the tie-dyed dress.

chapter six

Walking
the Dragon's Back

Justin grabbed his pack and began to race after Dax.

Then he stopped.

Abruptly.

Bearing right, the trail became a narrow ledge, running slightly upward along a vast section of open rock face. To the left now was a panoramic view of the horizon. On the trail above, Dax and the lady in the tie-dyed dress had already disappeared.

"You can do it, Justin," Jackie said. "Let me take the lead. I'll help you."

As Jackie made her way in front of Justin, Nick encouraged him. "Listen," he said. "This is it. This is the castle wall. The wall you said we had to climb to defeat the evil king. Come on, Justin, we can do this."

Before he could answer, Jackie took hold of his hand.

"Don't look down, Justin," she said. "Keep your head up and follow me."

Justin was filled with fear. But the thought of losing Dax scared him even more.

Leaning against the massive sheet of rock that tipped slightly away from the treetops below, the three Adirondack kids inched their way along the narrow ledge.

"This is a lot easier than I thought it would be," said Nick, who sounded like he was actually enjoying himself.

"It's still a little slippery from the rain this morning," Jackie warned. "Take your time."

Justin didn't say a word. Nick's confidence was encouraging, but not enough to persuade him away from fixing his eyes on the stone wall less than an inch from his nose. He slid his feet forward along the ledge and continued to hug the rock surface. Each arduous step was motivated by a single thought – Dax.

"Relax," Jackie said, suddenly. "We've made it." She turned to help Justin up beside her onto level ground. As he climbed up, he turned his head away from the rock face and into a furry one.

"Dax!" Justin said. He picked her up and squeezed her tightly.

"She just can't stay away from you for long, can she," said Nick, as he pulled himself up to join them. "That lady's talking probably drove Dax crazy."

"What do you think, Justin?" asked Jackie. "That was the hardest part of the whole climb. We're almost to the top now."

Justin turned and looked up the trail which was now transformed into a narrow ridge. Enveloped by tall spruce and fir trees, the arched and stony pathway appeared to wind its way through a tunnel of evergreens. "Well, we've come this far," he said. "We might as well go the rest of the way."

The sun was still high in the sky and continued to beat down on them.

"Hey, I'm thirsty," said Nick.

Jackie's eyes narrowed.

Nick's shoulders sagged. "Never mind," he said, and reached into his pack for a juice blaster.

Justin, Jackie, Nick and Dax continued their hike up the mountain. Temporarily sheltered by the trees, the walk was a little cooler.

As they traveled, Nick looked down at the trail, still solid stone. "Everything up here is rock," he said.

"That's why they call it Bald Mountain," said Jackie. "It's like the whole top of the mountain was scraped right off by a glacier."

Justin's curiosity was aroused. He stopped and looked down at his feet. "Hey, this isn't a trail at all," he said. "It's more like a spine."

"A what?" Nick asked.

"It's a spine," Justin said. "You know, like a backbone. We're not walking on a mountain right now at all. We're walking on the back of a dragon!"

"Then a glacier didn't scrape off the top of Bald

"My sword," Justin said.
He began to fence with Nick
on the back of the dragon.

Mountain," Nick said. "Everything was burned off by the dragon's fire."

"And he protects the evil king who built his tower on the top of the mountain," said Justin.

"Give me a break," Jackie said.

"We'd better get ready to fight the evil king," said Justin. He jumped off the dragon's back and picked up a loose stick from the ground. "My sword," he said, and climbed back up on the bumpy spine to fence with Nick.

"No fighting," warned Jackie. "We don't have time for this."

Nick had picked up a stick of his own and was ready for Justin's attack.

"We are not fighting," said Justin. "We're training." He swung his sword playfully at Nick, who countered with a fake block.

"Come on, Jackie," said Nick. "We're knights. You can be that famous girl knight, Joan of the Ark."

Jackie corrected him. "That's Joan of Arc," she said. "And the answer is no. Now let's go."

Justin bent on one knee and reached down to rub the dragon's back. "Feel his scales," he said. "They're all bumpy, like he has goose bumps."

"Maybe he's scared of us," said Nick, and laughed.

"Or maybe you're making him angry," said a voice from behind them.

chapter seven

A Chance Encounter

"Hi, I'm Nancy." The young girl reached out and shook hands with the three friends. "Are you guys headed up or down?"

Nancy looked like Jackie, except she was taller and had a lot more muscles.

"Up," said Justin. He could now imagine what Jackie would probably look like when she was older. "I'm Justin and these are my friends, Nick and Jackie." He flexed and rubbed his hand. "You sure have a strong grip."

Nancy smiled. "Well, it's a spectacular view at the summit," she said. "I can't believe I've never been up this mountain before. Are you working on your 23?"

"I've never heard of a 23er," said Justin, and pointed at Jackie. "But she wants to be a 46er."

Nancy looked at Jackie. "Oh, really? That's great. I'm a 46er, and I'm working on my 111 now."

Nick rolled his eyes. "46, 23, 111 – BINGO!" he said. "What's with all the numbers? There are more numbers to keep track of in mountain climbing than in math class."

Jackie jabbed Nick in the ribs. "There are 111 high peaks 4,000 feet or higher in New England," she explained. "But I've never heard of the 23, either."

"I guess it's kind of new," Nancy said. "It's the Forest Tower Challenge. It was created by the Glens Falls – Saratoga Chapter of the Adirondack Mountain Club."

"How does it work?" asked Jackie.

"You climb 18 of the 25 fire tower summits in the Adirondack Park and 5 in the Catskill Park," Nancy said. "When you've finished, you've met the challenge." She looked at Justin. "There is even a neat patch with a fire tower on it you could get for your bucket hat."

Dax walked over to the veteran climber and rubbed against her leg. Justin picked up his pet with his loose hand.

"What a gorgeous cat," Nancy said, and reached out to pet her.

"She's been following people today," Justin said. "And she seems to like you a lot."

"I do have to get going now," said Nancy. "By the way, Justin, is that a walking stick you are carrying?"

Justin's face flushed pink. "Um, no," he said, and gently tossed the branch back onto the ground among the trees."

"Well, nice meeting you," Nancy said. "Be careful along the trail, okay?" She took a few long strides, and was gone.

Nick looked at Jackie. Her head was buried in her hands. She was more flushed than Justin. In fact, she wasn't pink – she was fire engine red. "You're not sick now, are you?" he asked.

"I am so embarrassed," said Jackie. "Do you two have any idea who that was?"

"Let me take a wild guess at it," said Nick. "Ummm...Nancy?"

"Yes, Nancy," said Jackie. "Nancy Copeland! She is the whole reason I want to be a 46er. She climbed all 46 high peaks in one winter."

"In one *winter*?" said Nick. "Wow, she didn't look crazy."

Jackie ignored him. "And then when I finally get the chance to meet her in person, you guys are blocking the trail and playing with sticks like a couple of little kids."

Justin remembered now. So that was Nancy Copeland. Jackie had a magazine article that featured the young 46er cut out and taped to the side of her refrigerator.

"Maybe it wasn't her," suggested Justin, in an effort to make Jackie feel better. "I saw the picture from the magazine you have in your kitchen. The girl was all bundled up in winter clothes. How could you even recognize her?"

Jackie fired back quickly. "I just know it was her, okay?"

Justin slowly picked up his day pack and headed back up the trail with Dax at his side. The three friends walked along the ridge in single file, and in silence.

This adventure isn't working out at all like I hoped it would, Justin thought. *Things couldn't possibly get any worse.*

Of course, he was wrong.

chapter eight

Heads in the Clouds

"I think I see the tower," said Justin, excitedly.

Jackie ran up alongside him and peered ahead. "That's it," she said, and checked her watch. "We lost some time earlier, but if we hurry, we can still spend at least ten minutes on the top."

"I'm sorry, Jackie," said Justin, and shot a look at Nick.

"Yes, me too," said Nick.

"Forget it," Jackie said. "Let's get to the tower and have a good time the rest of the way. You two aren't going to believe what you'll be able to see."

The path widened and opened out onto enormous sections of barren rock. There were several lookouts along the way, but the three resisted the temptation to stop and stare, and pressed on until they reached the tower.

Justin's dad was right. Despite the early morning rain, the summit was a beehive of activity. And being Fourth of July weekend, American flags were everywhere. At first, Justin could not take his eyes off the fire tower. The large steel frame with a cab on top stood nearly 50 feet above him and people were moving up and down its five flights of open metal stairs in an effort to gain an even better glimpse of the mountains.

"Come over here, Justin," said Jackie. "Look."

He turned and froze. Not in fear, this time. In awe.

Stretched out directly below him and as far as he could see was a sea of green treetops. A horizontal slice of bright blue cut across the entire center of the landscape. It was the first section of the Fulton Chain of Lakes.

"It looks like a forest of broccoli growing down there," said Nick.

Jackie pointed far right. "There's First Lake," she said, and then slowly moved her finger to the left. "Then Second Lake, Third Lake and then our lake, Fourth."

"Hey, look at the little canoe," said Nick, pointing toward an object in a strip of water between Third and Fourth Lakes.

"That's not a canoe," Jackie said. "That's either the Clearwater or the Uncas."

"You can't mean the huge Cruise Boats," Nick said. "No way."

"I wonder if Captain McBride is out in the mail boat today," said Justin.

"He should be easy to see," said Nick. "Just look for a floating toothpick."

Patches of black dotted the landscape – shadows formed from the long, thin clouds that slowly altered shape as they drifted lazily through the sky.

Justin took off his pack and collapsed. He laid on his back and stared up at the easy moving clouds. Without any trees in his peripheral vision, it felt like he was floating in the air. His stomach tingled deep inside.

Jackie and Nick joined him, and the three friends lay side by side warmed by the sun from above and by the rock below that pressed against their backs.

"This is weird," said Justin. "It feels like we are moving instead of the clouds." He pulled his day pack under his head as a pillow. "What do you see?" he asked.

"Um...clouds?" said Nick.

"No, like do you see any animals or anything," said Justin. "Autumn clouds work better. There are a lot more puffy shapes. Hey, look at that one." He pointed upward. "It's a giant rabbit."

"You need a drink of water," Nick said. "You're delirious."

"Oh, I see it," Jackie said. "And it has a big, fluffy cotton tail."

"Okay, I get it," said Nick. "But that's not a rabbit's tail. It's a giant piece of popcorn."

They continued to lay quietly, carefully studying the evolving patterns above.

"I hate to say this," said Jackie. "I sure don't want to get you two started on that medieval stuff again."

"What?" asked Justin and Nick, together.

"Up there," she said.

"What?" they asked again, impatiently.

"I'm afraid to admit it," she said. "I definitely see...a dragon."

"Where?" asked Justin.

"There," Jackie said. She pointed to a large, uneven patch of white that stretched throughout the sky over a great distance.

"There is its head on the end of a long neck," she explained, and moved her finger like she was drawing in the air. "And see, the tail is curved and is even longer than the neck. It's kind of scary looking."

"I see it, now," said Justin. He didn't like that it had narrow eyes that seemed to be looking right at him. "It has four wings and there's even fire coming out of its mouth."

"Maybe it cooked the popcorn," said Nick. He didn't like the sinister form with its giant claws and gaping mouth, either. Squinting, he pointed in another direction. "Hey, what's that huge bird soaring way up there? Is it an eagle?"

Jackie reached into her pack and pulled out a field guide to birds. "Nope," she said, after flipping quickly through a few pages. "It's about the same size as an eagle, but judging from the shape, the head is too small and the tail is too long. I'd say it's a Turkey Vulture."

"A buzzard," said Nick. "Don't they just fly around dead things? They're creepy."

"And ugly," said Justin. "Vultures don't have any feathers on their heads. They're even balder than this mountain."

A slice of bright blue cut across the landscape.

"Yes, look at us," said Nick. "We're climbing Buzzard Mountain."

"They are not buzzards and they are not creepy," Jackie said. "I'll admit they aren't the most beautiful birds in the world, but they are important. Dead animals can become a public health hazard and so it's a good thing the vultures eat them. But they also eat other things like snakes and frogs and rodents."

"Like I said, they're creepy," said Nick. "And I'll bet there's something dead or dying right near here."

"Hey, where's Dax?" asked Justin, who had a difficult time taking his eyes away from the ominous dragon in the sky which still seemed to have its eyes fixed on him.

Nick quickly scanned the sky. "Sorry, Justin," he

It was the first section of the Fulton Chain of Lakes.

said. "I don't see any cloud up there that even begins to look like a cat."

Justin jumped to his feet. "No, the real Dax," he said. He looked all along the entire length of the rock face and then back toward the fire tower. There were plenty of people and day packs and water bottles and red, white and blue. But no cat.

Dax was gone, again.

chapter nine

Meow

"Excuse me," said Justin. He interrupted a small group of climbers who were seated together in a loose circle. "Did any of you happen to notice a cat walk by?"

Several of the people gave him a strange look, but before anyone could answer, a lone hiker standing nearby with a water bottle to his mouth waved him over with his free hand.

Jackie and Nick joined Justin in response.

The young man took another swig of water. "Yeah, I saw her," he said, and wiped his mouth with the back of his hand. "She sure is a nice looking calico. It's hard to ignore the first cat you've ever seen on a mountain, and I've climbed a lot of them." He pointed beyond the fire tower. "She took off that way."

Jackie sighed. "Great," she said, in dismay. "That path leads to a few good lookouts and then to nowhere. It's a dead end."

"Good," said Justin. "Dax will just follow the

path and she'll have to stop. It should be easy to catch up to her."

Jackie looked at her watch. "But we should be starting down the path to go back and meet Nick's mom right now," she said.

"Not without Dax," said Justin, and trotted off leading a reluctant Jackie and oblivious Nick toward the dead-end trail.

The clusters of climbers became thinner and the fire tower smaller as the trio slowly walked along, calling out to Dax.

"That's it," said Jackie. "No more trail."

"And no trace of Dax," said Nick.

Justin hung his head. "I should never have brought her up here," he said. He raised his head and his voice one more time. "DAX!"

Meow. The sound came from somewhere off the trail and downward, opposite the view of the Fulton Chain.

"It's Dax," said Justin.

"She sure sounds funny," said Nick.

"Well, maybe she's hurt," said Justin.

Meow.

"We should just stay on the trail," warned Jackie. "Let's keep calling her and maybe she'll come to us."

Meow.

"Not if she's hurt," said Justin. "I'm going."

Before Jackie could stop him, Justin plunged into the brush. Nick jumped in after him.

"Why do you do this to me?" shouted Jackie. Gritting her teeth, she fell in behind the two bush-whackers.

At first the stubborn shrubbery appeared randomly in small pockets, pushing out through crevices in the rock. But the further down and off the main trail the three friends moved, the denser grew the vegetation.

Meow.

"Where are you, Justin?" called Jackie. "Stay put for a minute."

"We're over here," he replied.

Jackie pushed through the brush to a small open spot on rock where Justin and Nick stood together, listening for another call from Dax.

"This is nuts," said Jackie.

Justin put his index finger up to his lips. "Shhhh – listen."

Meow.

"She keeps moving away from us," said Justin. "I don't get it."

Meow.

"Wait, that was real close," he said. "I think she's coming." He called out in his most persuasive and high-pitched tone of voice. "Come here, Dax. Here kitty, kitty."

There was a gentle movement low in the brush. A gray bird about the size of a robin and with a black cap, appeared on an open branch.

"Oh, brother," said Jackie.

44

"What?" asked Justin. He looked confused.

"That sound wasn't Dax," she said. "It was a catbird."

"A bird?" said Nick. "I told you that meow sounded funny."

Jackie pulled out her field guide again. "Yes, that's the sound a Gray Catbird makes when it's alarmed," she said. "There may even be a nest nearby."

"So, it was scared of us and started making that noise?" asked Justin.

"We startled it – or maybe he did," said Jackie. She pointed upward to a small boulder overlooking their position.

"A red fox," exclaimed Justin. The elusive mammal disappeared before he finished saying the word, 'fox'.

"That's unusual," said Jackie. "They are usually only out at night."

Justin felt a tingle in his stomach again. "That reminds me," he said, and hesitated. "What time is it?"

Jackie looked at her watch and her eyes widened. "Let's just say we are really, really late," she said.

The three Adirondack kids slowly turned in place to consider their surroundings. Leafy vegetation pressed in at eye level. Spruce and fir trees towered over them on all sides. There was no clear vision in any direction.

"I wonder where we are," said Justin. He turned to Jackie.

45

A Gray Catbird appeared on an open branch.

"Yeah, where are we?" echoed Nick. He, too, turned to their designated leader.

Neither of them liked the look in her eyes.

chapter ten

Lost & Found...
& Lost

Justin's legs felt weak. It was a sensation he remembered having only once before in his entire life. For a moment his mind left the mountains and he became a little boy again at the Carousel Mall in Syracuse.

Somehow he had lost sight of his parents one afternoon at the huge shopping complex. Pressed in on by strange people all around him in such a large and unfamiliar place, he was suddenly flooded with panic. He was dazed, confused and filled with fear. He found his mom's hand almost immediately. Or she found his. But he knew what it felt like to be lost. And it felt like he had been lost for an eternity.

"Justin, hey Justin." It was Nick, shaking his friend's shoulder to get his attention. "Are you all right?"

C'mon, you're almost eleven years old now, not a little baby, thought Justin. "Yeah, I'm fine," he said. He knew he sounded brave, or at least he thought he did. But he was still scared inside.

It was very quiet. Even the sound of cloth against cloth was exaggerated, the scratching noise obvious as Jackie slipped off her pack. "Here," she said, and handed Nick her thermos. "Just take a little drink and then hand it to Justin."

"This is really cold," said Nick. "I never knew water could taste so good."

Justin took a single, ice-cold gulp and then tipped his head. "Did you hear that?" he asked.

Jackie took the thermos from him and set it back into her pack. "No," she said.

"Listen, there it is again," said Justin. "It's like a mewing sound, but real soft. It's got to be Dax."

"Sorry," said Jackie. "This time we are staying put."

Nick agreed. "It's probably just that old catbird being chased by the fox," he said.

"It's definitely different than the bird," said Justin. "I've got to find out." And he was off again.

The brush was thick, and stubby branches kept slapping him in the face and legs. Sometimes they poked him in his side. He could hear his friends pushing through the tangle behind him, giving him the confidence to tramp on. This time the sound did not move away, and as he grew closer to the source, it became more distinct.

"Dax, is that you?" Justin asked gently, and pushed down several branches from a short pine tree. He stood amazed at his discovery and did not even feel Nick press up against his back to gawk over his shoulder.

Next came Jackie. "A baby," she gasped, and quickly pushed by Nick and Justin, both riveted in place.

"You were right, Justin, it wasn't the same sound," said Nick.

"Yoo hoo, yoo hoo, oh wonderful, wonderful. We are saved, sweet Sarah, we are saved." It was the lady in the tie-dyed dress. She was lying on her back next to her young daughter, and appeared unable to move much more than her head and arms. She only had one flip flop on, and one ankle was much larger than the other. And it was purple.

Jackie surveyed the situation and sprang into action. "Please don't move, ma'am," she said, then turned and motioned for the boys to secure the little girl.

"Mama, boo boo," said the little girl, as she stood up and pointed to her mother's large purple ankle.

Justin was amazed at Jackie's quick and decisive movements around the lady lying on the rocks, first urging her to lay perfectly still, then grasping the woman's wrist. She checked her watch.

"Are you feeling her pulse?" asked Justin.

"Yes," Jackie said. "And next is RICE for the ankle." She smiled at the little girl who had latched on to the bottom of Nick's shorts. "We're going to fix mama's boo boo."

"You brought rice in your pack?" asked Justin. "What didn't you bring?"

Nick offered to help. "Do we have to cook it?" he asked. "I'll build the fire."

50

"RICE stands for rest, ice, compression and elevation," Jackie explained, as she worked. "It's one of the first things we learned in first-aid to help people with an injury like this. Now hand me the thermos."

Within moments Jackie had the woman's leg slightly lifted up and resting in a splint made from the cloth child carrier. Ice from the thermos placed into a plastic sandwich bag was carefully wrapped to the swollen ankle.

"There's no broken skin," Jackie said. "It looks like a nasty sprain."

"Thank you, oh, thank you, thank you," repeated the woman over and over.

Justin waited for Jackie to stand and then made a hasty introduction. Little Sarah latched on to Nick's leg as the three Adirondack kids gathered around the large woman staring up at them from the ground.

"We saw you quite a ways back on the other side of the mountain," Justin said. "What happened?"

"Oh, my, yes, yes, forgive me, I never did introduce myself," said the woman. "My name is Penny. Please do call me Penny. I was born on Independence Day and every year I try to do something special to celebrate my birthday on the holiday. I had never climbed a mountain before and I heard this one was a wonderful walk for families." She stopped and looked down. "No, no, Sarah, no."

The toddler had half of a leaf in her hand. The other half was in her mouth.

"Yucky," said Nick, and took it from her hand. She frowned up at him. "Is it okay to give her a cookie?" he asked.

Sarah's face was transformed from a pout to a beaming smile. "Where cookies?" she asked. "Where cookies?"

Nick reached into his pack and took out several small pieces of animals: the leg of a bear, the beak of a loon, the head of a deer.

"Doggie woof," said Sarah, pointing to the deer without its antlers. In an instant it was gone. She held out her hand for more.

Justin laughed. "Hey, Nick, she can make those cookies disappear faster than you can."

"Excuse us, Penny," Jackie said. She bent to check her pulse again. "Please continue."

The woman in the tie-dyed dress explained she had heard there was another trail leading down the back side of Bald Mountain, and she decided to look for it.

"The pathway was quite narrow and slippery from the rain," Penny said. "I lost my balance and hugged my Sarah to protect her as we tumbled down through the bushes. And now you have come to save us."

Justin grimaced. Before he could say anything, Jackie stood and took him by the arm. "Come over here a second, will you, Justin?"

The two stepped a few feet away.

"What is that awful look on your face?" she

whispered. "Don't say anything right now about being lost."

"I wasn't going to," replied Justin. He grimaced again. "I just want to know...what is that *smell?*"

chapter eleven

A Tower of Strength

Justin, Jackie and Nick followed their noses and were led to sweet little Sarah. With wet cookie crumbs in her hands, she reached up for Nick, blinked her bright green eyes and broke a smile through a face covered with pale blue frosting.

"Oh, my Sarah needs to be changed," said her mother, and laughed. "There are clean diapers and tidy-wipes in the bag that dropped out of my hand as I stumbled."

Nick's face flushed. He looked at Jackie with a pleading look in his eyes.

"Why are you looking at me?" asked Jackie. "And don't say it's because I am a girl."

The thought of Nick changing a dirty diaper sent Justin into hysterics. He couldn't stop laughing.

"What's so funny?" Jackie asked. "We're drawing sticks for it."

Justin sobered up immediately. "I vote Nick does it," he said, quickly. "Sarah really likes him." It had never occurred to him that among their many hands, his might be anywhere near the frightful job.

Jackie held up a clenched fist holding three small twigs, just their teeny, tiny tips sticking up all even in a row.

Nick drew first, and smiled. His twig was shorter than an inch worm. "Beat that," he said to Justin.

Jackie turned to face him. "You're next," she said.

Justin studied the two remaining tips carefully. He had no idea which one might be longer. He shrugged his shoulders and plucked the one on the right from her fist. There seemed no end to it. He slowly pulled and pulled until he held a stick the width of Jackie's entire hand.

She smiled and opened her fist to reveal a third twig even shorter than Nick's.

Justin moaned.

"You two stay right here," Jackie said. She looked up in the general direction of the woman's fall and noted several broken branches in small bushes that betrayed the path of her tumble downward. "I'll be right back."

Justin looked calm on the outside. But inside, his mind was reeling. *How can this be happening?* he thought. *First Dax is lost. Then we are lost. And even if we find our way back to the trail, I'm stuck on a mountain that I don't even know if I can get back down. And now on top of it all, I have to change a disgusting, dirty diaper.*

"I'm back," said Jackie. She exploded through the bushes. "I didn't find the main bag, but I did find two diapers in a small plastic bag and the tidy-wipes. They must have spilled out when the carry bag went loose and turned over." She handed every-thing to Justin.

Somehow the process wasn't as bad as he had imagined. Coached by Sarah's mother while hold-ing his breath, he was finished in a matter of moments.

Nick was the one laughing now, but stopped abruptly as Jackie handed him the plastic bag con-taining the discarded diaper.

"You had the second shortest twig, right Nick?" she said, and smiled. "You know the rules of the wilderness – take nothing but pictures, leave noth-ing but footprints." Nick held the plastic bag at arm's length with his fingertips and slowly deposit-ed it into his day pack.

"What time is it?" asked Justin.

Jackie checked her watch. "We are really, really late now," she said, and looked up at the sun. It was still hot. They were all tired now, still thirsty and beginning to get hungry for some real food.

Justin began to worry again, but then looked down at Sarah's cheerful face. He smiled and placed his bucket hat on her head. The back brim of the hat touched her shoulders. "Now you won't get a sunburn," he said.

"Mama walk," Sarah said.

"Mama can't walk right now," said her mother, who had become a lot less talkative. She looked at the Adirondack kids. There was now a look of concern in her eyes. "Will one of you be going for help now, or all three of you?"

Jackie was about to confess they, too, were lost when Justin surprised even himself with a sudden burst of courage. "Well, none of us quite yet," he said. "You see, we were looking for my cat, Dax, when we found you. So, if you're kind of feeling all right, Jackie and I are going to look around a little more for my cat. We'll be right back."

Jackie looked amazed. "Where did that come from?" she asked Justin, as they walked slightly out of sight.

"I don't know," said Justin. He felt a surge of confidence well up inside of him. "We have to do something. And I have to find Dax. I'm not leaving this mountain until I find her. Didn't you see the trail at all when you looked for that bag?"

Jackie nodded. "Not even a hint of it," she said. "But it must be right nearby. She couldn't have fallen that far down or she would have been hurt a lot worse."

"Then let's go find it," said Justin. "And keep an eye out for Dax. She would blend in really easy down here."

"We can't," said Jackie. "We've already moved more than we should have. Nancy Copeland has walked up 46 high peaks in the middle of the winter and never once got stuck where she had to stay overnight. I can't believe I might have to stay up here all night on my very first trip without my parents, but staying put is the right thing to do."

Overnight on the mountain? Justin thought. *No food – no water – no tent?* "I know I messed up bringing Dax," he said. "But I did bring a few other things."

"Like what?" Jackie asked.

Justin's day pack was limp without Dax inside. He reached into one of the bag's tiny compartments. "Like the whistle you told me to bring," he said, and held it up. "We can take turns blowing on it. Maybe someone will hear it and find us."

"Not bad," said Jackie. "Let's go back and give it a try."

Nick was relieved to see his friends return. "I'm running out of cookies," he said. "But I still have a lot of candy."

"Where candy?" asked Sarah, and reached out with her hand. "Where candy?"

"Oops," said Nick.

Jackie looked at Penny who did not appear well. "I'm sorry, but we seem to have lost the trail. We may have to spend the night here," she announced. "Justin brought a whistle. We'll take turns blowing it and try to attract some attention."

Justin put the whistle to his lips and sounded out several long, shrill notes.

"Wait a minute," said Nick. He was stunned and there was panic in his voice. "We can't stay up here all night." Movement in the sky caught his attention. "Look, it's the vulture," he said, and dropped to the

58

ground on his knees. "I knew it, we're goners."

And then the phone rang.

chapter twelve

A Royal Rescue

Everyone stared at Nick's day pack.

"You brought a phone?" Jackie asked.

It rang again.

"Answer it," said Justin, excitedly.

Nick needed no encouragement. Still on his knees, he pawed his way wildly through candy bars, candy wrappers, band-aids, video game cartridges, cookie crumbs and one plastic bag with a dirty diaper all the way to the bottom of the pack and grasped the ringing life line.

"Hello?" he said. "Hi, mom." He cupped his hand over the receiver and looked at Jackie and Justin. "It's hard to hear – there's a lot of static."

"Yes, mom, yes," he continued. "What are we having for dinner?"

"What are we having for dinner?" Justin repeated, in disbelief. "Are you crazy? Tell her where we are. Tell her what's going on!"

"Quiet," Nick said. "I can't hear."

Justin reached out for the phone, and Nick pulled

away. The phone slipped from his hand and smashed into pieces against the stony surface at their feet.

"Great, just great," said Justin.

"It's your fault," said Nick. "Why didn't you leave me alone?"

Justin was indignant. "We're stuck up here and you're asking your mom what you're having for dinner?"

Jackie interrupted. "Excuse me, children," she said, sarcastically. "Nick, what did your mother say?"

Nick scowled at Justin. "She said we're having barbecued chicken."

Justin shook his head and sat down on a boulder.

"Is someone coming for us?" asked Penny, hopefully.

"I'm not sure," said Nick. "It was kind of hard to hear. Mom said she put the phone in my pack last night after I went to bed so we'd have it in case there was an emergency."

"Well, let's start blowing the whistle again," said Jackie.

Nick shook his head and pointed at Justin. "I am not putting my mouth on that whistle after he's slobbered all over it."

Justin ignored him and began to check his pockets. "Where is my whistle, anyway?" he asked.

A shrill sound pierced the air. Then another. And another.

"Okay, thank you, Sarah," said Jackie. "Now give me the whistle."

The little girl continued to blow the whistle in short bursts as she moved in a small circle flapping her arms and avoiding Jackie's grasp. Her short brown hair bounced as she ran.

"Shhh, I hear something," Justin said. He pointed to the tops of several small trees and some bushes that were moving about vigorously a short distance away.

"Maybe it's the fox," whispered Nick.

"Not the way those trees are moving," said Jackie, softly. "It's something a lot bigger."

"Maybe it's a bear," said Nick. He began searching the sky nervously. "You don't see that vulture again, do you?"

"Everyone quiet," whispered Justin, sternly. "It's coming closer." He pointed behind them. "Look, more treetops are moving over there."

The rustling in the branches of the trees and brush grew louder and louder all around them.

Nick squeaked. "Maybe it's a pack of coyotes," he said.

"I wish we had some real swords now," said Justin.

Jackie picked up little Sarah and carried her to her mother's side.

The five lost hikers huddled together in a small heap gathered around the woman in the tie-dyed dress.

There was a crackling sound from the trees.

"I see them just ahead." It was a female's voice from somewhere behind them, loud and bold.

A man dressed in green with a walkie-talkie in his hand stepped out into the clearing. "Thanks, I see them now."

Justin jumped to his feet. "Ranger Bill!" he said. Bill Buck was not only the region's forest ranger, he was also a good neighbor and friend of Jackie's family.

"Your folks were a little worried about you," said the ranger. "It was smart to have a solid plan." He looked at the woman and small child. "What have we here?"

"Oh, these wonderful, wonderful young people found me and helped me after I took a nasty fall," the woman said. Her bubbly voice had returned. "My name is Penny and they watched after my little princess."

"Princess?" Justin said. "Did you say, *princess*?" He looked at Nick who was already looking at him.

"Why, yes, yes," said the woman. "That is what the lovely name, Sarah, means – it means, princess." She hugged her daughter tightly. "We're rescued," she said.

"So we saved a princess after all," said Justin.

Nick smiled broadly.

Jackie rolled her eyes.

"Hi, Nancy," said Ranger Bill.

Everyone turned as another figure stepped out into the clearing from the small pine trees behind them.

"Folks, this is Nancy Cope –," started Ranger Bill.

"We've met," said Jackie, before he finished his introduction.

"Hi, you guys," said Nancy. She looked down at the woman's ankle. "Wow, nice job on the splint. Whose work is it?"

"Jackie did it," said Justin. "She's the best out-doors woman I've ever known."

Nancy looked at Jackie approvingly, and smiled. "Hey, you can climb with me anytime," she said.

Jackie blushed. "Thanks," she said.

Ranger Bill kneeled to examine the woman's ankle and spoke briefly into his walkie-talkie. Then he stood and addressed the group. "Okay, folks, a copter is on its way," he said. "We'll have a support team here very soon to help transport Penny back to the top of the mountain."

"A copter," said Justin. "Do you mean a helicop-ter? A real helicopter?"

"That's right," said the ranger. Then he looked toward Nick and grimaced. "What in the world is that *smell*?"

chapter thirteen

Where's Dax?

The helicopter was loud. Real loud.

The three adventurers weren't as far from the main trail as they had imagined, and it hadn't taken long for the forest rangers from Otter Lake, Boonville, Blue Mountain Lake, Stillwater and Raquette Lake to converge on the fallen hiker. Assisting members of the Eagle Bay, Inlet and Old Forge Fire Departments, the rangers strapped the lady in the tie-dyed dress onto a large, flat board and using a series of ropes, hoisted her back up to the summit of Bald Mountain. The Adirondack kids helped by standing clear of the rescue operation.

Little Sarah still clung to Nick as the olive green craft, shaped like a giant grasshopper, hovered high above them. A large red cross was visible on its side.

"I can't believe how many people it takes to save somebody on a mountain," yelled Justin to his friends.

A small crowd had gathered to witness the event. "Stand way back," called Ranger Bill, and motioned in an exaggerated manner with his hands and arms for everyone to move far away from a large, flat open space where the helicopter would attempt to touch down. Only a few emergency medical personnel and four rangers were near the landing spot. They surrounded the flat board which still held the injured woman.

Nick poked Justin in the back to get his attention, but the noise grew deafening as the helicopter descended upon the summit.

Justin could see Nick's lips move, but couldn't hear anything above the helicopter's relentless whine. The spinning blades moved around so fast, they seemed invisible. He pointed to his own ears, slowly mouthed the words, I – can't – hear – you, and shrugged his shoulders.

There wasn't enough space for the helicopter to set down firmly. With one skid on the mountain and the other suspended off the rocky ledge in mid-air, the pilot held the craft steady as the rangers lifted the woman through a wide side door that resembled the small mouth of a cave.

One of the rangers emerged from the opening and ran toward the Adirondack kids. He gently lifted little Sarah into his arms and returned to the helicopter quickly. Then they, too, disappeared inside.

Ranger Bill gave the pilot a thumbs up, and as the giant green craft with a red cross moved upward and away, the small crowd erupted into a round of thunderous applause.

"Dax!" Justin cried, and ran
for the fire tower's first flight of metal stairs.

"Justin," said Nick, and poked him again.

"What?" asked Justin, annoyed at being poked over and over while trying to concentrate on the drama unfolding before them.

"Look," said Nick, and pointed up toward the cab at the top of the fire tower.

Justin leaned his head back and squinted. He could make out the silhouette of a small creature with four legs standing on the ledge of the large open window. "Dax!" he cried, and without hesitation ran for the first flight of metal stairs. He grabbed the rail and tore quickly up the steps, passing people at each platform who were on their way down.

"What a cute cat," he heard someone say, as he turned to take the second flight of stairs.

"Are you sure it wasn't a raccoon?" he heard someone else say, and made the turn for flight number three.

He was met at flight number four with, "I've never heard a cat cry so much."

Moving slower now from sheer exhaustion, he pressed on.

Flight number five was empty. Each metal step resounded under his feet like exclamation points emphasizing his resolve to reach his beloved companion.

And then, a dead-end. He was greeted by a solid ceiling of wood planks. No one was allowed to enter the cab above. A small trap door was padlocked shut – the only entrance now, a slim broken hole in the floorboards.

Justin gasped for air and swallowed hard. "Dax," he called, in a high-pitched voice. "Here, kitty, kitty, kitty, kitty. C'mon, girl. Where are you?"

Nothing.

He tried again.

"C'mon, Daxy," he called. "Treat. Treat." He didn't actually have a treat to give her, but this was an emergency.

There was a dull thump on the floor above, and then two green eyes peered at him through the hole.

Meow. Dax reached with a paw through the opening in the floor.

"How did you even get up there, girl?" Justin asked.

"Does it really matter?" It was Jackie, with Nick huffing and puffing right behind her. "Ranger Bill is waiting for us. Let's just get her down."

Jackie was the tallest, but still not tall enough to reach Dax. "One of you will have to get down on all fours to give me a lift," Jackie said.

"Let's shoot odds and evens for it," said Nick.

"Forget it," said Justin. He dropped down to his knees and planted his two hands onto the platform. Nick held Jackie steady as she used Justin for a stool and reached up for Dax.

"She's not there anymore," said Jackie, her feet digging into Justin's back.

"Here, kitty, kitty," said Justin, and groaned. "Please, Daxy. C'mon, girl."

Jackie jumped down. "It's no use, it's not working," she said.

"Maybe we can both hold Justin," offered Nick.

"In the air?" Justin shook his head vigorously back and forth. "No way."

Jackie bent forward and cupped her hands together. "Come on, Justin," she said. "Put your foot in here. I'll lift you up to call her. Dax will only come to you."

"I'm not sure..." said Justin.

"That's a maybe, and maybe is..." started Jackie.

"I know, I know," said Justin. "And maybe is, yes." He raised his leg and planted his foot into the hand-made stirrup. Nick pushed on his friend's backside as Jackie lifted, thrusting him upward. Jackie stumbled slightly and Justin felt himself sway in the air. He saw the mountains, then the ground, then the mountains again as his flailing arms reached up for the ceiling to steady himself.

"I – can't do this – very long," Jackie said, the strain apparent in her voice.

"C'mon, Daxy," Justin said again, the palms of his hands now braced against the wood ceiling. His free leg swung back and forth and helped him achieve some balance.

The cat appeared in an instant at the sound of Justin's voice and squeezing through the small hole, dropped headlong into the top of his open pack. "Got her," he cried, and Jackie lowered them both in a rush. Nick made sure his friend landed upright.

They could all feel the vibration in the platform from the sudden impact of the falling weight.

Justin pulled Dax from his pack and buried his face in her neck.

"Wow, look at the mountains from up here," Nick said.

"There it is," said Jackie, and pointed toward the northeast horizon.

Nick quickly scanned the clouds. "Not another dragon," he said. "You know what happened the last time you saw a dragon."

Jackie laughed. "No, over there," she said. "It's Mount Marcy, the highest peak in the Adirondacks. And I'm going to climb it some day."

So preoccupied with rescuing Dax, it hadn't even occurred to Justin to take a good look from the top of the tower. He slowly shifted his feet and turned to share the view. Shadows were beginning to stretch out across the chain of lakes as the sun moved lower in the sky. His breath was even, his stomach was calm and his heart wasn't pounding any more. In fact, he liked what he was feeling, standing there at the top of the world. He sighed. "I think the dragon is gone for good, Nick," he said, and smiled. "Let's go home."

chapter fourteen

In Plane View

THE ANNUAL FOURTH OF JULY WEEKEND PING PONG BALL DROP at Inlet was one of the community's most anticipated holiday events. Hundreds of children lined up in Fern Park and waited to gather handfuls of colorful balls that were dropped through the air from a plane. Each coded ball falling from the sky represented a prize to be picked up in the park pavilion.

A bright yellow seaplane rocked in the blue waves at the Roberts' dock on Fourth Lake as the three Adirondack kids climbed aboard for their historic flight.

"Is it true you have to fly upside down to let out all the ping-pong balls?" Nick asked the pilot, as he scrambled into a small blue padded seat next to Justin at the rear of the plane.

The question caught the pilot by surprise and he laughed out loud. Nick frowned at Justin, who already had his safety belt on in the seat right next to him. "I'm sorry, son, I've never heard of such a thing." He showed Nick a handle located on the floor in front of him. "We are just a few minutes from the park. I'll let you know when to pull this lever and release the balls."

Jackie climbed in last and sat in a seat in front of the boys and directly behind the pilot. She was very quiet.

"Hey, why are there parachutes back here?" asked Nick, as the pilot settled into his own seat and turned on the engine.

Jackie looked back at him. "They are not parachutes," she said, and rolled her eyes. "They're life jackets."

The roar of the motor was deafening, and from where the three friends were seated, it was even louder than the helicopter the day before.

"Life jackets?" Nick yelled to be heard. "Why do we need life jackets?"

The plane turned away from the dock and began moving across the surface of the water toward Cedar Island. The engine grew louder as the plane picked up speed. The pontoons began banging against the waves.

"I think I changed my mind," yelled Nick.

Justin ignored him. He watched out the window at the water splashing near the bottom of the vibrating plane. It felt like they were moving over a relentless series of speed bumps. He thought it was kind of scary, but exciting.

The island appeared closer and closer until the speed bumps abruptly ended, and the island before them dropped from sight. The Adirondack kids were airborne.

Nick turned around and glanced out the back window.

"What are you looking for?" yelled Justin.

"My stomach," yelled Nick.

The seaplane made an easy arc in the sky banking left to get into position for the low pass over Fern Park.

Jackie was still unusually quiet.

Nick nudged Justin. "I wonder if someone else is finally scared of heights?" he yelled, and pointed to her sitting in the seat in front of them.

Justin kicked him and motioned for him to leave Jackie alone.

The pilot turned his head slightly sideways. "Pull the lever when I say the word, 'now'," he yelled back to the boys.

Nick looked at Justin. "What did he say?"

"He said to pull the lever when he says, 'now'," yelled Justin.

"Now?" yelled Nick.

"Yes, 'now'," yelled Justin.

Nick reached out and pulled the lever.

"No, not now," yelled Justin, and grabbed for his arm.

Nick frowned. "You said, 'now'," he yelled.

It was too late. A rainbow of red, yellow, blue, purple and orange ping-pong balls streamed through the sky from the bottom of the plane.

A rainbow of red, yellow, purple, orange
and blue ping-pong balls streamed
through the sky from the bottom of the plane.

The colorful shower was over in seconds as the balls dropped into the boats of fishermen and popped off the roofs of camps all along the northern shoreline of Fourth Lake.

epilogue

There was a whistle and a flash of light from the edge of Cedar Island. Then a bang and a burst of color sprayed out onto the black canvas of the evening sky.

The fireworks were awesome. They always were.

Justin sat on the dock in the dark with Nick and Jackie and all their parents. He watched as the light revealed silhouettes of boats on the water underneath the aerial show and reflected onto the faces of his two friends sitting next to him.

Nick began to sing. "And the rahhh–ckets red glare, the bombs burrrs–ting in air..."

It was awful, but no one complained.

Jackie simply sat with her legs crossed, and each time the light faded, searched for shooting stars.

Dax was hiding in the kayak in the boathouse. Justin still didn't know how she got into that cab at the top of the fire tower on Bald Mountain.

He supposed that would always be a mystery.

And he didn't know how climbing that tower somehow took away his fear of heights.

He supposed that would always be a mystery, too.

 DAX FACTS

There were once nearly 70 **fire towers** at the tops of mountains in the Adirondack and Catskill Parks. The fire tower at Bald (Rondaxe) Mountain dates back to 1917 and is one of just 23 left in the Adirondacks. The Department of Environmental Conservation abandoned the towers when it was determined nearly all fires were being reported by private citizens. Several groups are working to restore some of the towers for recreation and education. The *Fire Tower Challenge* was created by the Glens Falls – Saratoga Chapter of the Adirondack Mountain Club. Climb the summits and earn a patch. Learn more in *Views from on High – Fire Tower Trails in the Adirondacks and Catskills* by Freeman with Haynes, published by The Adirondack Mountain Club, Inc.

Justin at Bald (Rondaxe) Mountain fire tower, Adirondack Park

Photograph by Gary VanRiper

 **DAX FACTS**

Photograph by Gary VanRiper

Can't climb a mountain? The **1919 observation tower from Whiteface Mountain** is on exhibit at the **Adirondack Museum** at Blue Mountain Lake. Featuring 23 indoor and outdoor exhibits on 32 acres, the Adirondack Museum was called "the best of its kind in the world," by the *New York Times*. A great family destination with many interactive programs and historical displays, it is one of the authors' favorite places to visit in the Adirondacks again and again. For more information visit www.adkmuseum.org.

Photograph by Gary VanRiper

The **Gray Catbird** has the ability to mimic the calls of other birds, but is named for its distinct catlike mew. About the size of a small robin, the catbird has a body, wings and tail that are slate gray and has a black bill and cap. A small chestnut patch appears near its tail. Common throughout New York state, the species has managed to penetrate the lower spruce-fir forests of the Adirondacks. Many campers have been lured into the woods upon hearing the catbird's call to look for "the poor lost little kitty", only to return from their search in vain.

SUGAR COOKIE RECIPE

1½ cups powdered sugar
1 cup margarine or butter, softened
1 teaspoon vanilla
½ teaspoon almond extract
1 egg
2½ cups all-purpose flour*
1 teaspoon baking soda
1 teaspoon cream of tartar
Granulated Sugar

Mix powdered sugar, margarine, vanilla, almond extract
and egg. Stir in remaining ingredients except granulated sugar.
Cover and refrigerate at least 3 hours.

Heat oven to 375 degrees. Divide dough into halves.
Roll each half ³⁄₁₆ inch thick on lightly floured cloth-covered board.
Cut into desired shapes with 2 – to 2½ inch cookie cutters;
sprinkle with granulated sugar. Place on lightly greased cookie sheet.
Bake until edges are light brown, 7 to 8 minutes.
About 5 dozen cookies; 65 calories per cookie.

If using self-rising flour, omit baking soda and cream of tartar.

DECORATING SUGAR COOKIES: Omit granulated sugar.
Frost and decorate cooled cookies with creamy vanilla frosting
tinted with food color if desired. Decorate with colored sugar,
small candies, candied fruit or nuts if desired.

CREAMY VANILLA FROSTING

3 cups powdered sugar
⅓ cup margarine or butter
1½ teaspoons vanilla
About 2 tablespoons milk

Mix powdered sugar and margarine. Stir in vanilla and milk;
beat until smooth and of spreading consistency.

Reprinted by permission. Betty Crocker Cookbook. Golden. Pages 112 & 77.

About the Authors

Gary and Justin VanRiper are a father and son writing team residing in Camden, New York of the Tug Hill region along with their family and cats, Socks and Dax. They spend many summer and autumn days at camp on Fourth Lake in the Adirondacks.

View from Bald Mountain

The Adirondack Kids® began as a short writing exercise when Justin was in third grade. Encouraged after a public reading of an early draft at a Parents As Reading Partners (PARP) program in the Camden Central School District, the project grew into a middle reader chapter book series. *The Adirondack Kids*® *#2* is their second book.

About the Illustrators

Glenn Guy is an award-winning political cartoonist who lives in Canastota, New York. *The Adirondack Kids*® *#2* is his second book.

Susan Loeffler is a freelance illustrator who lives and works in Central New York. *The Adirondack Kids*® *#2* is her second book. loeffler_sl@yahoo.com

The Adirondack Kids® #1

Justin Robert is ten years old and likes computers, biking and peanut butter cups. But his passion is animals. When an uncommon pair of Common Loons takes up residence on Fourth Lake near the family camp, he will do anything he can to protect them.

The Adirondack Kids® #2
Rescue on Bald Mountain

Justin Robert and Jackie Salsberry are on a special mission. It is Fourth of July weekend in the Adiron-dacks and time for the annual ping-pong ball drop at Inlet. Their best friend, Nick Barnes, has won the opportunity to release the balls from a seaplane, but there is just one problem. He is afraid of heights. With a single day remaining before the big event, Justin and Jackie decide there is only one way to help Nick overcome his fear. Climb Bald Mountain!

All on sale wherever great books on the Adirondacks are found.

The Adirondack Kids® #3
The Lost Lighthouse

Justin Robert, Jackie Salsberry and Nick Barnes are fishing under sunny Adirondack skies when a sudden and violent storm chases them off Fourth Lake and into an unfamiliar forest – a forest that has harbored a secret for more than 100 years.

The Adirondack Kids® #4
The Great Train Robbery

It's all aboard the train at the North Creek station, and word is out there are bandits in the region. Will the train be robbed? Justin Robert and Jackie Salsberry are excited. Nick Barnes is bored – but he won't be for long.

Also available on **The Adirondack Kids®** official web site

www.ADIRONDACKKIDS.com

Watch for more adventures of The Adirondack Kids® coming soon.

The**Adirondack Kids**® #5
Islands in the Sky

*Justin Robert, Jackie Salsberry
and Nick Barnes head for the
Adirondack high peaks wilderness –
while Justin's calico cat, Dax,
embarks on an unexpected tour
of the Adirondack Park.*

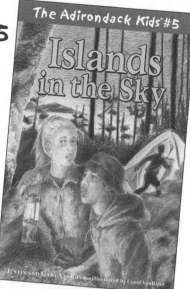

The**Adirondack Kids**® #6
Secret of the Skeleton Key

*While preparing their pirate ship
for the Anything That Floats Race,
Justin and Nick discover an antique
bottle riding the waves on Fourth
Lake. Inside the bottle is a key
that leads The Adirondack Kids to
unlock an old camp mystery.*

Over
60,000
Adirondack Kids
Books in
Print!

All on sale wherever great books
on the Adirondacks are found.

Watch for more adventures
of The Adirondack Kids® coming soon.